GW00808901

Stories taken from *The Helen Oxenbury Nursery Story Book*
first published 1985
This edition published 1995 by William Heinemann Ltd
an imprint of Reed Consumer Books Ltd
Michelin House, 81 Fulham Road, London SW3 6RB
and Auckland, Melbourne, Singapore and Toronto
Text compilation and illustrations
© Helen Oxenbury 1985, 1994, 1995

ISBN 0 434 974137

Printed in Italy

£2
002418

HELEN OXENBURY
First Nursery Stories

Contents

Little Red Riding Hood 6

Goldilocks and the Three Bears 13

The Three Little Pigs 21

HEINEMANN

Little Red Riding Hood

There was once a little girl whose mother made her a new cloak with a hood. It was a lovely red colour and she liked to wear it so much that everyone called her Little Red Riding Hood.

One day her mother said to her, "I want you to take this basket of cakes to your grandmother who is ill."

Little Red Riding Hood liked to walk through the woods to her grandmother's cottage and she quickly put on her cloak. As she was leaving, her mother said, "Now remember, don't talk to any strangers on the way."

But Little Red Riding Hood loved talking to people, and as she was walking along the path, she met a wolf.

"Good morning, Little Girl, where are you off to in your beautiful red cloak?" said the wolf with a wicked smile.

Little Red Riding Hood put down her basket and said, "I'm taking some cakes to my grandmother who's not very well."

"Where does your grandmother live?" asked the wolf.

"In the cottage at the end of this path," said Little Red Riding Hood.

Now the wolf was really very hungry and he wanted to eat up Little Red Riding Hood then and there. But he heard a woodcutter not far away and he ran off.

He went straight to the grandmother's

cottage where he found the old woman
sitting up in bed. Before she knew what
was happening, he ate her up in one gulp.
Then he put on the grandmother's
nightdress and her nightcap, and climbed
into her bed. He snuggled well down under

the bedclothes and tried to hide himself.

Before long, Little Red Riding Hood came to the door with her basket of cakes and knocked.

"Come in," said the wolf, trying to make his voice sound soft.

At first, when she went in, Little Red Riding Hood thought that her grandmother must have a bad cold.

She went over to the bed. "What big eyes you have, Grandmama," she said, as the wolf peered at her from under the nightcap.

"All the better to see you with, my dear," said the wolf.

"What big ears you have, Grandmama."

"All the better to hear you with, my dear," answered the wolf.

Then Little Red Riding Hood saw a long nose and a wide-open mouth. She wanted to scream but she said, very bravely, "What a big mouth you have, Grandmama."

At this the wolf opened his jaws wide.

"All the better to eat you with!" he cried. And he jumped out of the bed and ate up Little Red Riding Hood.

Just at that moment the woodcutter passed by the cottage. Noticing that the door was open, he went inside. When he saw the wolf he quickly swung his axe and chopped off his head.

Little Red Riding Hood and then her grandmother stepped out, none the worse for their adventure.

Little Red Riding Hood thanked the woodcutter and ran home to tell her mother all that had happened. And after that day, she never, ever, spoke to strangers.

Goldilocks and the Three Bears

Once upon a time, there were three bears who lived together in their own little house in the wood. There was a great big father bear, a middle-sized mother bear, and a little baby bear. They each had a special bowl for porridge, a special chair for sitting in, and a special bed to sleep in.

One morning the mother bear made their porridge for breakfast and poured it out into the great big bowl, the middle-sized bowl, and the little baby bowl. But it was so hot the bears decided to go for a walk while it cooled.

Now a little girl called Goldilocks was walking in the woods that morning and she came across the bears' house. She knocked on the door and when there was no reply, she crept slowly in.

"Oh! Oh!" she cried when she saw the bowls of porridge. "I'm so hungry; I must have just one spoonful."

First she went to the great big bowl and took a taste. "Too hot!" she said.

Then she went to the middle-sized bowl and tried that porridge. "Too cold," she said.

Last she went to the little baby bowl. "Oh! Oh! Just right!" she cried, and she ate it all up, every bit.

Then Goldilocks saw the great big chair and climbed into it. "Too big," she said, and climbed down quickly.

Next she went to the middle-sized chair and sat down. "Too hard," she said.

Then she went quickly to the little baby chair. "It just fits," she said happily. But really the chair was too small for her and - CRACK - it broke, and down she tumbled.

Then she went into the next room where she saw three neat beds. First she climbed into the great big bed, but it was too high. Next she climbed into the middle-sized bed, but it was too low.

Then she saw the little baby bed. "Oh! Oh!" she cried. "This is just right." She got in, pulled up the covers, and went fast asleep.

Before long the three bears came home for their breakfast. First the great big bear went to eat his porridge.

He took one look and said in his great rough voice, "Somebody has been eating my porridge!"

Then the middle-sized bear looked into her bowl and said in her middle-sized voice, "And somebody has been eating my porridge, too!"

Finally the little baby bear went to his bowl. "Oh! Oh!" he cried in his little baby voice. "Somebody's been eating my porridge and has eaten it all up!"

After that, all three bears wanted to sit down. The great big bear went to his great big chair and saw that the cushion had been squashed down. "Somebody has been sitting in my chair," he cried in his great big voice.

Then the middle-sized mother bear went to her middle-sized chair and found her cushion on the floor. "Somebody has been sitting in my chair," she said in her middle-sized voice.

Then the little baby bear hurried to his chair. "Oh! Oh!" he cried in his little baby voice, "Somebody's been sitting in my chair and broken it all to bits!"

The three bears, feeling very sad, went into the bedroom.

First the great big bear looked at his bed. "Somebody has been lying in my bed," he said in his great big voice.

Then the middle-sized bear saw her bed all rumpled up and she cried in her middle-sized voice, "Oh dear, somebody has been lying in my bed."

By this time the little baby bear had gone to his little baby bed and he cried, "Somebody has been lying in my bed, and she's still here!"

This time his little baby voice was so high and squeaky that Goldilocks woke up with a start and sat up. There on one side of the bed were the three bears all looking down at her.

Now Goldilocks did not know that they were kind bears and she was very frightened. She screamed, jumped out of bed, ran to the open window, and quickly climbed out. Then she ran home to her mother as fast as she possibly could.

As for the bears, they put things to rights, and since Goldilocks never came again, they lived happily ever after.

The Three Little Pigs

Once there were three little pigs who grew up and left their mother to find homes for themselves.

The first little pig set out, and before long he met a man with a bundle of straw.

"Please, Man," said the pig, "will you let me have that bundle of straw to build my house?"

"Yes, here, take it," said the kind man.

The little pig was very pleased and at once built himself a house of straw.

He had hardly moved in when a wolf came walking by and, seeing the new house, knocked on the door.

"Little pig, little pig," he said, "open up the door and let me in."

Now the little pig's mother had warned him about strangers, so he said, "No, not by the hair of my chinny-chin-chin, I'll not let you in."

"Then I'll huff and I'll puff and I'll blow your house down!" cried the wolf.

But the little pig went on saying, "No, not by the hair of my chinny-chin-chin, I'll not let you in."

So the old wolf huffed and he puffed and he blew the house down, and ate up the little pig.

The second little pig said good-bye to his mother and set out. Before long he met a man with a bundle of sticks.

"Please, Man," he said, "will you let me have that bundle of sticks to build my house?"

"Yes, you can have it. Here it is," said the kind man.

So the second little pig was very pleased and used the sticks to build himself a house. He had hardly moved in when the wolf came walking by and knocked at the door.

"Little pig, little pig," he said, "open up your door and let me in."

Now the second little pig remembered what his mother had told him, so he, too, said, "No, not by the hair of my chinny-chin-chin, I'll not let you in."

"Then I'll huff and I'll puff and I'll blow your house down!" cried the wolf.

But the little pig went on saying, "No, not by the hair of my chinny-chin-chin, I'll not let you in."

So again the old wolf huffed and he puffed, and he huffed and he puffed. This time it was much harder work but, finally, down came the house and he ate up the second little pig.

Then, last of all, the third little pig set out and met a man with a load of bricks.

"Please, Man," he said, "will you let me have that load of bricks to build my house?"

"Yes, here they are – all for you," said the

kind man.

The third little pig was very pleased, and built himself a brick house.

Again the wolf came along, and again he said, "Little pig, little pig, open your door and let me in."

But like his brothers, the third little pig said, "No, not by the hair of my chinny-chin-chin. I'll not let you in."

"Then I'll huff and I'll puff and I'll blow your house down!" cried the wolf.

And when the third little pig wouldn't open the door, the wolf huffed and he puffed, and he huffed and he puffed. Then he tried again but the brick house was so strong that he could not blow it down.

This made the wolf so angry that he jumped onto the roof of the little brick house and roared down the chimney, "I'm coming down to eat you up!"

The little pig had put a pot full of boiling water on the fire and now he took off the lid. Down the chimney tumbled the wolf and - SPLASH - he fell right into the pot.

Quickly, the little pig banged on the cover and boiled up the old wolf for his dinner.

And so the clever little pig lived happily ever after.